BAD BOYZ

2

Leagues Apart

The Bad Boyz series

1 **Kicking Off**

Take seven children (six boys and a girl) who are always in trouble. Add a teacher who offers to form them into a football team in the local little league. What do you get? Bad Boyz!

2 **Leagues Apart**

Bad Boyz are starting their first season in the Appleton Little League. They look good in their new strip and they're playing well. But trouble is never far away and a falling-out threatens to pull the team apart...

3 **K.O. Kings**

Bad Boyz are one of the favourites to win the Appleton Little League Cup. But then trouble strikes in the shape of goalie Kyle's dad. And now something's up with skipper Dareth too. Is this a K O for Bad Boyz cup dreams?

4 **Barmy Army**

As Appleton Little League Champions, Bad Boyz have been invited to take part in a mini tournament in France. Everyone's very excited – except Sadiq. What will Bad Boyz make of France – and what will France make of them?

Bad Boyz

Leagues Apart

Alan Durant

ReadZone Books Limited
50 Godfrey Avenue
Twickenham
TW2 7PF
UK

First published in this edition 2014

© Alan Durant 2001
© in this edition ReadZone Books 2014

First published 2001 by Walker Books Ltd

Alan Durant has asserted his right under the Copyright Designs
and Patents Act 1988 to be identified as the author of this work.

Graphics and cover design: Jurian Wiese
Design: Nicolet Oost Lievense
Images: Shutterstock

Printed in Malta by Melita Press

British Library Cataloguing in Publication Data (CIP) is available
for this title.

ISBN 978 178322 446 3

Visit our website: www.readzonebooks.com

For all the players, parents, managers, dogs, etc., who turn up for Little League football every Saturday morning

1

'Wow!'

'Cool!'

'Wick-ed!'

The brand-new football shirt, held up by Mr Davies, received the loud approval of his team. In their only game so far, Bad Boyz had played in a strip borrowed from their school. Now, for their first match in the Appleton Little League, they were to play in their very own kit. The shirt displayed by the manager even had the team's name emblazoned across it in big black letters: **BAD BOYZ**. It also bore the name of their sponsors: the Doorstep Dairy.

'Max's dad has done us proud,' said Mr Davies as he handed round the new shirts. Max's dad was a milkman with the Doorstep Dairy and he'd managed to persuade his employers to pay for his son's team's strip. The dairy's chairman was a keen football fan and liked to support local ventures.

'We're gonna look like Brazil!' said Dareth, the Bad Boyz captain, holding his shirt up in front of his chest. The shirt was a bright custard yellow.

'Yeah!' squeaked Andrew, alias Bloomer, the smallest member of the team. His shirt hung down almost to his knees.

'Hey, look, Bloomer's got his nightie on,' laughed Jordan, the team's only girl.

'Just as long as he doesn't go to sleep in the game,' said Mr Davies pointedly.

Bloomer was famous for his tiny attention span. It frequently got him into detention at school – where, in the past at least, he had regularly been joined by the rest of the team. It wasn't for nothing that they were called Bad Boyz.

When they were dressed, Mr Davies called them round for a team talk. He glanced around to check they were all there: Dareth, Sadiq, Jordan, Bloomer, Sung-Woo, Kyle....

'Max!' he called. 'Where are you?'

Right on cue, Max appeared from the toilet – wearing his dark blue shorts on his head.

'You called, master?' he boomed, as if he were

a genie summoned from a magic lamp. The others laughed.

'Max,' Mr Davies sighed, 'put your shorts on your backside and let's get this show on the road. We've got a match to play.'

Max bowed low. 'Yes, master,' he intoned. He took the shorts off his head, grinning hugely.

Finally, all the team were fully dressed and ready for action.

'Right,' said Mr Davies. 'This is a big day for us, isn't it?'

'Mmm.' There was a general murmur of agreement.

'We've come a long way in the last couple of months,' the coach continued. 'Now we've reached our goal. We're going to play in the little league. Well, you are, anyway. I'll just be watching from the sidelines. I've done my bit, now it's up to you.' He paused to glance around the semicircle of children in front of him. His mind returned to that day in early spring when, fed up with seeing the same seven children in detention all the time, he'd suggested the idea of forming them into a football team. Now, here they were, looking every centimetre a team in their new yellow and blue strip....

A loud fart brought these fond thoughts to a sudden end. There were groans of disgust.

'Kyle!' Sadiq accused.

Kyle, the team's goalkeeper, was a picture of wobbly innocence.

'Me?' he protested. He frowned so hard, his small eyes almost disappeared into his pale face like raisins into a bowl of porridge.

'I didn't do nuffing! It was Sung-Woo.'

'I think we'd better get out in the open,' said Mr Davies, 'before we're all gassed.'

His players needed no second invitation. At once, the room echoed with the sound of studs tapping and clumping their way across the wooden floor.

Only Sung-Woo remained. His face, as ever, bore a serious, slightly baffled expression.

'Is no gas,' he said gravely. 'Is just my bottom. I have too many beans for breakfast. Beans make you f –'

'Yes, thanks, Sung-Woo,' Mr Davies interjected. 'It's your feet I'm interested in. Now, off you go and get kicking that ball. I want to see some goals from you today.' Sung-Woo was the team's striker.

'Yes, sir,' he said – and he almost smiled.

2

Bad Boyz first opponents were Vinnie's Vulcans. They were already out on the pitch in their green and white shirts and green shorts. They were practising their shooting when Bad Boyz ran out of the changing room. A small ginger-haired boy flicked a ball into the air and volleyed a shot past his keeper, high into the back of the net.

'He looks all right,' said Dareth appreciatively.

'Nah,' said Kyle. 'I'd've saved that easy.' He stretched out a meaty arm, miming a save.

'You'd never have got near it, you big jelly,' said Sadiq. He and Kyle often had a go at each other. In the past at school their arguments had frequently led to blows and, later, detention. Since Bad Boyz had come together, though, they'd managed to get on – most of the time.

'You don't know nuffing,' Kyle huffed.

Mr Davies arrived just in time. 'Hey, you're on the same side, you two,' he chided. 'You'll boost the other team's confidence if they see you arguing among yourselves. Now let's get warmed up....'

Warming-up was Bad Boyz least favourite activity and they always met its announcement with a collective grumble. But Mr Davies insisted on it. Before their twice-weekly training sessions and now before this first match against the Vulcans they went through a rigorous routine of bends, stretches, jogs, jumps and sprints. Only then did they get to kick a ball around.

They divided in half, forming two straight lines with the front players, Dareth and Sadiq, facing each other. Mr Davies threw Dareth a ball and the exercise started. Dareth passed the ball to Sadiq then sprinted across to the back of the opposite line. Sadiq trapped the ball and passed to the new front player in the other line, Sung-Woo. Then Sadiq sprinted to the back of the opposite line. And so it went on, until everyone had received and passed the ball five times.

After that they practised shooting. Again they stood in a line. This time the front player was Jordan. She passed to Mr Davies, who was standing midway between her and Kyle in goal. Mr Davies tapped the ball to his left, while Jordan ran on and shot first time. The ball whizzed wide – much to Kyle's amusement.

'You wanna get some glasses, Jordan,' he laughed.

'You want to get a brain, Kyle,' Jordan retorted.

'Just get the ball, Jordan,' said Mr Davies.

Kyle was good at this exercise and very difficult to beat. He wasn't the most agile of keepers, but he made full use of his size to block the shots that were on target. He let in only a couple of goals from the many shots fired at him.

'It's like trying to get past the Incredible Hulk,' moaned Sadiq, as Kyle pulled off yet another comfortable save.

'Well, let's hope the Vulcans feel like that too,' said Mr Davies. 'I don't want any silly goals going in our end. Let's try to keep a clean sheet. OK, Max?'

'Sir!' Max shouted, raising his hand to his

head in a military salute. Then he toppled sideways to the ground.

Mr Davies smiled. Max loved to clown around now, but when the whistle blew for the match to start he'd be the most competitive player on the pitch. It was a transformation that never ceased to amaze all those who knew him.

And just at that moment, the whistle did indeed blow for the captains to go to the centre circle for the toss of the coin. Dareth walked forward for Bad Boyz and the ginger-haired boy for Vinnie's Vulcans. The referee introduced himself, then asked the two captains to shake hands.

'Right, who's going to call?' he asked.

'I will,' said the ginger-haired boy quickly. He called 'heads'. It was.

'We'll have kick-off,' he said. 'Which end do you want?'

'We'll stay as we are,' said Dareth. He grinned. 'Our keeper don't like to move much.'

The ginger-haired boy looked past Dareth to where Kyle was sitting on his goal-line. Then he grinned too. 'Don't worry,' he sneered. 'All he'll have to do is turn round ... to pick the ball out of the net.'

Dareth shook his head. 'He don't like to do that neither,' he said.

The other boy snorted. 'Sounds like he doesn't like to do anything.'

'Yeah, he does,' Dareth contradicted him. 'He likes to squash ginger nuts.'

With that he turned and walked back to take up his place for the kick-off.

3

Vinnie's Vulcans had about a dozen supporters. Bad Boyz had one – and that was Mr Davies.

Max's dad had hoped to come, but the dairy was short-staffed and he had to do a second milk round. The other mums and dads were either working or had other commitments on a Saturday morning. Some, like Dareth's, had gone AWOL.

Mr Davies did his best to make himself heard, but he felt like a tinkly triangle in a band of trombones. The Vulcans manager, Vinnie, was particularly loud. He had a rough deep voice which he made full use of – bellowing instructions and criticism, between chomps on his chewing gum.

'Shaun, get your finger out!'

'I said run, Ryan. A snail could do better than that!'

'Oi, what're you two doing back there? Havin' a tea party?'

'Kieron, if I wanted you on the left wing, I'd've put you there! Now get back and defend!'

These shouts were usually echoed by one or more of Vinnie's fellow supporters, which meant there was barely a quiet moment.

It was pretty hectic on the pitch too.

It was the first league match for both sides and they played as if it might be their last. The tackling was strong and there was fierce competition for every ball. Sometimes too fierce. After one clash between Sadiq and Ryan, the ginger-haired boy, the referee took them both aside and warned them to cool down.

Vinnie wasn't impressed. 'Come on, ref, it's a man's game!' he grunted, almost swallowing his gum. As it happened, the player closest to him was Jordan. She turned and glared and for a minute or two Vinnie went silent.

'Come on, Bad Boyz!' Mr Davies called, taking advantage of the rare lull.

So far his team had done well, especially as they were playing into the breeze. With five minutes to go in the first half, the score was still 0-0 and there was little to choose between the teams. The Vulcans had had more of the ball, but apart from a couple of good shots from Ryan, they hadn't created any real chances. At the other end, Dareth had a shot cleared off the line following a corner. At half-time 0-0 would be a good score, Mr Davies reckoned. But it wasn't to be.

An attack by the Vulcans ended with the ball rolling harmlessly out of play for a goal kick. As Vinnie shouted in disgust at his players, Kyle placed the ball on the line at the edge of his goal area. Glancing around, he saw Bloomer unmarked just outside the penalty box. Quickly, he kicked the ball towards him. However, at that moment, a large plane flew overhead and Bloomer's attention went with it.

'Bloomer!' Kyle yelled. But by the time Bloomer reacted, Ryan had stepped in and stolen the ball. Sadiq and Max had pushed too far forward and the Vulcan captain had a clear run on goal. As Kyle moved out to meet him, Ryan dragged the ball back, flipped it up and, just as he had in practice, volleyed it powerfully into the net. Kyle had no chance.

'YES!' cried the Vulcans' supporters.

Vinnie was overjoyed. He took a last chomp on his gum then spat it out, as if he were casting away all his cares.

'That's the way, Vulcans!' he bellowed. 'Now, let's get another!'

'Never mind, Bad Boyz. Heads up!' Mr Davies urged. But his voice was lost amid the celebrations around him.

4

At half-time, the score was still 1-0, though Ryan had come close to putting the Vulcans further in the lead. This time his shot had hit the post and Max had cleared the rebound.

'Told you you wouldn't save his shot, didn't I?' Sadiq grumbled to Kyle as the team gathered gloomily for their oranges.

'It weren't my fault,' said Kyle. 'It was Bloomer, weren't it? He weren't lookin'.'

'Yeah, well, you still didn't save the shot, did you?' Sadiq persisted.

'Joe Hart wouldn't have saved that shot,' Dareth pointed out.

'That's right,' Mr Davies agreed. 'Kyle's doing fine – and so are you all. There's no need to be down. We can still win this one, especially now we've got the wind behind us. They've only got one really good player, but he's getting too much space. Max, I want you to mark him, OK? Everywhere he goes, you go too. If we can stop that Ryan playing, then they'll struggle.'

The peep of the referee's whistle summoning the teams for the second half was followed by a deafening roar from Vinnie.

'Here we go, Vulcans! Hundred miles an hour!' he rasped before chomping on a new stick of gum.

'I wish someone could stop *him*,' Jordan complained, putting her hands over her ears.

'A couple of goals should do it,' said Mr Davies. He smiled encouragingly at his striker. 'Eh, Sung-Woo?'

Sung-Woo frowned. 'I try,' he said. Then he farted. 'Sorry,' he apologised as the others swiftly moved away to take up their places on the pitch.

'Well, you've certainly got the wind behind *you*, Sung-Woo,' Mr Davies remarked, before retreating to the touch-line.

The second half began as competitively as the first. Jordan made a couple of tackles that had Vinnie roaring with outrage, though the referee saw nothing wrong. He did blow his whistle for a foul, though, when one of the Vulcans tripped

Dareth. 'You gotta be jokin', ref!' Vinnie howled.

The referee ignored him.

Mr Davies waved his players forward. 'Let's have a big kick into the area, Sadiq,' he urged.

Sadiq did as his coach instructed. He booted the ball towards the Vulcans' goal. It was a strong kick but the wind made it even stronger. The ball soared into the air and only started to drop when it had gone over the heads of the players gathered in the penalty box. The Vulcans keeper dived to his left, but couldn't reach the ball which, to everyone's surprise, bounced against the post and into the net. Bad Boyz had equalised.

'Yes!' Now it was Mr Davies's turn to celebrate. Vinnie, meanwhile, put his head in his hands.

'I – you- er,' he spluttered, before lapsing into glum silence.

Sadiq's team-mates ran to congratulate him. For once, he was happy. He didn't lose his smile even when Kyle shouted to him that the goal was a fluke.

'Who cares?' he shrugged – and no one argued.

For a while the game was close with neither side making any clear chances. But the Vulcans were tiring. They were starting to have difficulty getting out of their half. When they did, Max and Sadiq were waiting for them. Max was superb. He followed Ryan like a lanky Rottweiler, snapping in to make a tackle whenever the Vulcan captain got the ball. As a result, Ryan lost heart and drifted out of the game – much to his manager's annoyance.

'Pull your finger out, Ryan, or I'll drop you next week!' Vinnie bullied, but his words only made Ryan more dejected. Mr Davies felt sorry for the boy. In the end, though, it wasn't the Bad Boyz coach or a Vulcan team-mate who stood up for Ryan; it was Sadiq.

'Why don't you shut up?' he yelled at Vinnie finally, after the Vulcan manager had bellowed yet another threat at his star player.

Vinnie nearly swallowed his gum. He looked as if he might explode.

'Oi, you little toe-rag!' he exclaimed at last when he'd stopped coughing.

Mr Davies was about to say something when

the referee intervened.

'Right, that's enough! Any more outbursts like that and I'll ban you from the touchline,' he warned the Vulcans' manager.

'Come on, ref!' Vinnie protested. But now even his fellow supporters turned on him and told him to give it a rest. This was too much for Vinnie. He threw up his hands with an angry 'humph' and walked away.

Later he was probably glad he did, because he wouldn't have liked what followed one bit: Bad Boyz scored with their very next attack. Dareth and Jordan played a neat one two, then the captain beat the last defender and walloped the ball into the net.

For the last ten minutes it was one-way traffic. Sung-Woo went close, Dareth hit the bar, Jordan rattled a post. Then Bloomer went on a scampering run down the left, leaving two opponents in his wake before crossing the ball to Sung-Woo. His shot went straight at the keeper, but the ball rebounded to Dareth, who smashed in his second goal. Ryan, who'd perked up a bit since his manager had departed, did pull a goal back minutes later, but the Vulcans were a beaten team. Sung-Woo added a fourth goal for Bad Boyz and soon after the referee blew his whistle for the end of the game. Bad Boyz had won their first game in the Appleton Little League four goals to two.

5

The Appleton Little League had a magazine.
It was called Top Shots and contained news,
results and match reports from the league. Mr
Davies brought in a copy to show his players
in the week after their second match – against
Dorking Runners, which they won 5-2. There
was a report on the match by the league
secretary, Stan Reynolds. Mr Davies read it out.
His team were not impressed.

'Is that it?' Max scoffed. 'That was pants.'

'Kyle could've written a better report than
that and he's a moron,' Sadiq remarked.

'Me gran's budgie could've written a better
report than that,' Dareth added.

'That bloke don't know nuffing,' Kyle
grumbled.

'He was more interested in his half-time pie
than the match,' huffed Jordan.

'Who ate all the pies, who ate all the pies,'
Max sang. 'You fat b-'

Mr Davies raised his hand. 'All right, Max, enough,' he ordered. He stared hard at his team. 'Now look, you lot, if you think you can do better, why don't you?'

'Eh?' said Sadiq.

'What do you mean?' Jordan queried.

'I mean that you should produce your own match report,' Mr Davies continued. 'Take it in turns to write it, maybe. You could use one of the computers in the ICT suite.' He nodded at Jordan. 'You're an artist, Jordan. You could design a heading and some graphics. We could put the report up on the school notice-board – and send a copy to the league too.' He smiled. 'Show them how it should be done.'

Jordan shrugged. 'OK,' she said, as if she didn't really care one way or the other. 'But I don't want anyone else interfering.'

'We could put in the results and league tables too,' Dareth suggested.

Jordan scowled. 'I'm not doing that,' she muttered. 'That's numbers and stuff.'

For the first time Sung-Woo spoke. 'I do that,' he said simply.

'Yeah, Sung-Woo's wicked at maths and he's sick on the computer too.'

Sung-Woo looked baffled. 'I no sick,' he uttered.

'I mean you're very good, brilliant,' Max explained. 'Sung-Woo helps me with my maths homework sometimes and I help him with his English.' Sung-Woo smiled and nodded. Max contorted his face ridiculously. 'How now brown cow?' he pronounced comically.

'Very useful if you need to have a conversation with a cow,' Mr Davies remarked.

'Well, his dad is a milkman,' Dareth pointed out.

'Ah, yes, that reminds me,' said Mr Davies. 'We should send a copy of the match reports to the dairy too. You'd better put their name at the top, Jordan: Bad Boyz, sponsored by the Doorstep Dairy.'

'I'm not drawing any cows, though,' Jordan grouched.

The first official Bad Boyz report appeared just over a week later. The author was Max.

But Max being Max, he couldn't just write the report, he had to make it sound as if he was actually commentating on the game.

BAD BOYZ
Sponsored by the Doorstep Dairy

BAD BOYZ VS DART UNITED
MATCH REPORT
BY 'MAD' MAX DRISCOLL

Hi, folks!
This is Mad Max reporting on the top Appleton Little League clash between the fabulous Bad Boyz and their opponents Fart United. Sorry, I mean Dart United!

Bad Boyz kick off and go on the attack. Sung-Woo taps the ball to Dareth. He kicks the ball back to Sadiq, who boots it out to Bloomer. He passes the ball back to Dareth. He goes past one player, then another. He shoots! He ... misses! Only joking. He scores! Bad Boyz take the lead in the first minute. Amazing! The crowd go wild. 'One Dareth Clements, there's only one Dareth Clements!' they sing. Oh no, that's not the crowd singing, it's Dareth!

Dart United don't know what's hit them. Bad Boyz are all over them. Sadiq and Max are having a blinder. They're unbeatable. And behind them there's Kyle: Mount Everest in goalie gloves.

Now Jordan's got the ball. She runs at the Dart United defence. She crosses the ball to Sung-Woo. He goes past the last defender as if he wasn't there. He shoots. He scores! 2-0! What a goooooooooal! Is that a smile I can see on Sung-Woo's face? Yes, I do believe it is. Sung-Woo has smiled, ladies and gentlemen. How about that?

It's all Bad Boyz now. Dart United may as well go home, 'cos Dareth's just knocked in a third. 3-0 at half-time! Who'd have thought it? These Bad Boyz are out of this world. Look at them suck those oranges. They're on fire!

The second half is like the first half – only it comes after it. Bad Boyz attack like demons. Jordan scores, then Sung-Woo scores, then Dareth scores. Kyle makes a great save. Bloomer spots a helicopter. Sadiq goes on a run and wins a corner. Is there no end to the excitement, folks? No. Well, not for Max anyway, 'cos when the corner comes over, he leaps like a flying wombat and heads the ball into the net. It's the goal of the match! It's the goal of the season! Is there no end to this boy's talent? To find out, you'll just have to read next week's Bad Boyz match report.

This is 'Mad' Max Driscoll saying, 'Goodbye and goooooooood riddance!'

6

Mr Davies was very pleased with the report. As he pointed out to the less enthusiastic head-teacher, Mr Fisher (alias Piranha), in making the reports his players had to use ICT, literacy, numeracy and design skills – and it kept them out of trouble.

'Yes, I suppose you're right,' Piranha replied. 'But lavatories aren't on the school curriculum, so please ask your players to cut the toilet humour. I really don't want that sort of language on the school notice-board. I don't know what the Ofsted inspectors would say.'

'Outstanding?' Mr Davies suggested, then exited quickly before Piranha could respond.

The next two reports were by Sadiq and Kyle each recording Bad Boyz victories. Mr Davies read the reports before they went on display, removing some of the more dodgy comments – such as Sadiq referring to one referee as a 'cow pat on legs', or Kyle calling an opposition striker 'a fat turd'. Mr Fisher, Mr Davies explained to his players, would not be impressed.

Before each report was the current league table, carefully updated by Sung-Woo, who was given the complete set of results every Monday morning by Mr Davies. This is how the table stood after the first five weeks:

Teams	Played	Won	Drawn	Lost	For	Against	Points
Bad Boyz	5	5	0	0	25	7	15
Terminators	5	3	1	1	21	5	10
Vinnie's Vulcans	5	3	1	1	18	8	10
Hornets	5	2	3	0	18	7	9
Dorking Runners	5	2	2	1	11	11	8
Eddy's Eagles	5	1	1	3	11	13	4
X Club 7	5	0	0	5	2	22	0
Dart United	5	0	0	5	1	34	0

'You're doing really well with those tables, Sung-Woo. Keep it up,' Mr Davies enthused.

'It's easy,' said Sung-Woo. 'I show you if you like.'

'Why don't you show us all?' Mr Davies suggested.

Sung-Woo shook his head. 'They say they no

interested in numbers.'

'I bet they all know how many goals they've scored, though,' said Mr Davies.

A small smile dimpled Sung-Woo's cheeks. 'But Kyle no want to know how many he let in,' he remarked.

'No,' his manager agreed. 'I bet he doesn't.'

With five weeks gone and Bad Boyz top of the table, everything was going as smooth as syrup. But with Bad Boyz, trouble was never far away.

The bubble burst the very next game. Bad Boyz were beaten 2 -1 by one of their main rivals, Hornets. It was the first ever defeat they had suffered and they were as sick as the sickest parrots.

After the match Mr Davies tried to lift his team. They were unlucky to lose, he said, but he was sure that the defeat would make them stronger and more determined.

Then came the match report. It was a few days late because Jordan wrote it and she was, as many of her teachers had remarked, a very reluctant writer. If she could have drawn or tagged the report it would have been produced a lot faster. It was Thursday lunchtime when Jordan read her report out to the others - and she left no one in any doubt who she held to blame for the Bad Boyz defeat.

'Bad Boyz were set for a good draw when Bloomer made a stupid mistake in the very last minute. Max made a great tackle and passed the ball out of defence to Bloomer. As usual Bloomer wasn't paying attention. He was looking at a dog running along the touch-line. Jordan shouted but it was too late. The Hornets striker got the ball and scored an easy goal. Thanks to Bloomer, Hornets won.'

'You can't put this up on the noticeboard, Jordan,' said Mr Davies when he read the report. 'You've got to pull together after a defeat. Blaming one another won't do anyone any good.'

'But it *was* his fault,' Jordan argued.

'Yeah, it were,' Kyle agreed. He pointed a chunky finger at Bloomer. 'You should've been lookin'.'

'I *was* looking,' Bloomer squeaked.

'Yeah, but the wrong way,' Kyle insisted.

Bloomer's pink cheeks went bright scarlet. 'Well, you're stupid,' he squawked. 'You're all stupid. And I'm not playing anymore.' Then he ran out of the room.

No one knew quite what to make of this. As a rule Bloomer was one of the more easy-going members of the team. If it had been Kyle or Sadiq or Jordan who had stormed out no one would have turned a hair. But Bloomer? His reaction took everyone by surprise.

'I'll see if I can find out what's wrong,' said Mr Davies.'Meanwhile, Jordan, change that report....'

Mr Davies had a busy timetable that afternoon and he wasn't able to seek out Bloomer until the end of the day. But Bloomer had already gone.

'He ain't been here all afternoon,' Dareth informed him. 'I think he must've gone off after that argument with Jordan.'

Mr Davies frowned. 'I wonder what's up with him?' he pondered.

'I'll go round and see him if you like,' Dareth offered brightly. 'I'm his mate. He'll tell me.'

'Good idea,' Mr Davies said. 'Come and find

me at lunchtime tomorrow.'

He was relieved by Dareth's suggestion. The Bad Boyz skipper may have had a talent for getting into trouble, but he was generally good-humoured and well-liked by his peers. If anyone could take the heat out of the situation, it was most likely Dareth. Mr Davies hoped so anyway. Bad Boyz next match was only two days away and it was their most important yet: the top of the table clash with Terminators. The winners would be declared champions for the first half of the season. And that wasn't all. The chairman of the Doorstep Dairy, Bad Boyz kit sponsors, was coming for the first time to watch....

7

Dareth's face was unusually sombre when he found Mr Davies at lunchtime the following day.

'He ain't comin' into school,' he pronounced grimly, 'and he ain't gonna play tomorrow neither.'

'What's the matter with him?' Mr Davies asked.

Dareth rubbed his shaved scalp with a grimace as if he'd touched a sore. 'His mum's ill. She's been sick and 'avin' stomach cramps and all. Bloomer's scared she's gonna die.'

'Die!' Mr Davies exclaimed. 'Why does he think that?'

''Cos she's got to go into hospital.'

'Lots of people go into hospital for tests. It doesn't mean they're going to die,' Mr Davies said calmly.

'Well, Bloomer reckons she is,' said Dareth. He reflected for a moment. 'Oh and he said he ain't gonna play for Bad Boyz again unless Jordan apologises for saying it was his fault we lost against 'ornets.'

Mr Davies sighed. 'Well, we can ask her,' he said dubiously.

Dareth shook his head. 'She won't,' he said.

'We'll have to try anyway,' Mr Davies insisted. 'Let's have a team meeting in my room at the end of school.'

As the school emptied for the weekend, six members of Bad Boyz duly turned up in Mr Davies's room. Their silent gloom was in stark contrast to the excited bustle in the corridors outside. Mr Davies began by stating the Bloomer situation, though they'd all heard it from Dareth anyway.

'So, Jordan, what do you think about apologising?' the manager asked tentatively.

Jordan glowered. 'For what?' she huffed. 'I only told the truth.'

'She did,' Kyle insisted.

Mr Davies tried a different tack. 'Look, everyone makes mistakes,' he said reasonably. 'You're not telling me surely, Jordan, that you did everything right on Saturday? Or you, Kyle?'

'Me?' Kyle glooped.

'Yeah,' Sadiq interjected. 'You could have done better with their first goal. You fell over like a hippo on ice.'

'I slipped in the mud!' Kyle responded hotly. 'Anyway, if you'd tackled that bloke he wouldn't 'ave been able to shoot, would he?'

Mr Davies clapped his hands. 'Ok, that'll do!' he said sternly. 'I think my point's been made, don't you?' Jordan still didn't look convinced. 'Look, we all know Bloomer's concentration isn't the best. But that's the way he is. And right now he needs our support. Imagine if your mum had to go into hospital, Jordan, you'd want the others to be sympathetic, wouldn't you?'

'I suppose,' Jordan muttered with her usual reluctance.

'And there's a practical side to this too,' Mr Davies continued. 'Tomorrow we've got our biggest game of the season – and we don't want to go into it a player down, do we?'

'No,' Jordan conceded.

'So, you're prepared to apologise?' Mr Davies pushed.

Jordan shrugged. 'I suppose,' she mooched again.

'Good,' Mr Davies enthused. 'Perhaps you could write a short note. In fact why don't we send Bloomer a card to say we're thinking of him? You can all sign it and Dareth can give it to him tonight.' Mr Davies was full of enthusiasm now. 'I've got a card I keep in my desk for emergencies.'

'I hope it don't say 'appy Birthday!' said Dareth.

'Or 'Congratulations on passing your driving test',' Sadiq added.

'Or 'Be My Valentine'.' Max breathed dramatically, pretending to swoon. The others laughed.

Mr Davies smiled too. 'It doesn't say anything. It's blank for any occasion,' he informed them. He found the card and they all wrote a few words of encouragement (the gist being 'We hope your mum gets better soon and please come and play tomorrow') and signed it. For her part, Jordan just wrote 'Sorry'.

'You don't waste words, do you, Jordan?' Mr

Davies observed, to which Jordan replied with her usual shrug. He hoped that single word would satisfy Bloomer. But he knew better than to push Jordan any further. He sealed the envelope and wrote 'Bloomer' on the outside, then he handed it to Dareth to deliver.

'We'll just have to hope for the best,' he said. 'Cross your fingers and touch wood.'

Max crossed his fingers - and his eyes - and tapped his head twice.

Sung-Woo spoke for the first time. 'I no understand. Why do we cross our fingers and touch wood?'

'It's good luck,' Mr Davies explained.

'Ah, hangunul bengenyo,' Sung-Woo nodded.

'Eh?' gawped Kyle.

'I wish you 'good luck' in Korean,' Sung-Woo explained. He pulled out a chain from beneath his shirt. It held a yellow metal pendant with red symbols on it.

'This is my pujok, my lucky charm,' he said with a shy smile.

'Well, let's hope it works,' said Mr Davies. 'We need all the good luck we can get.'

Dareth started to move towards the door. He waved the envelope he was holding in the air. 'Hang an earl Big Ben yo,' he grinned. Then he walked out.

8

It was a perfect morning for football. The sun beamed down warmth and goodwill on the world.

In the Bad Boyz changing room Mr Davies waited for his team to arrive. It was always a bit nerve-wracking this wait, wondering if some new trouble would have struck overnight and prevent one or more of his players from coming to the game. This morning the manager was especially anxious.

One by one the players trooped in: Sadiq, Max, Sung-Woo, Kyle, Jordan... Then Dareth arrived – but there was no sign of Bloomer. The captain shook his head mournfully.

'I gave 'im the card and he was well pleased,' he said. 'But then he started crying. An ambulance took his mum into 'ospital. She had terrible pains and Bloomer says he's sure she's gonna die.' He made a gesture of helplessness with his hands. 'I told him what you said, sir, about the tests and all, but he wouldn't 'ave it. He said he was too upset to play and anyway he needed to be at home in case there was any news from the 'ospital.'

Mr Davies sighed deeply. 'Poor Bloomer. Ah well, you did your best, Dareth. We'll just have to manage with six today.'

Slowly and silently the Bad Boyz players got changed into their football kit. Mr Davies watched them with deep concern. This match would be hard enough if all his players were their usual perky, energetic selves, but in their present heavy, downcast mood he feared the worst. Somehow he needed to lift them. But how? What could he possibly say or do that might bring the usual excited glow to their faces? What could anyone do? He glanced at his watch. There were only ten minutes to kick-off. They should have been outside warming-up by now.

'All right, everyone,' he said, willing some words of inspiration to enter his muddled brain. 'Listen up. I know that - '

Wheee! The door to the changing room

swung open behind him. He turned and was amazed to see Bloomer, standing in the doorway.

'I'm here!' he announced, his voice half gasp, half squeak. 'I've come to play!'

As he looked around, seven pairs of eyes stared back at him like they were viewing a ghost.

'Bloomer!' Mr Davies exclaimed at last. 'You're here.' He spoke uncertainly as if he were trying to believe it might be true. Meanwhile, the others continued to stare at Bloomer as if they definitely didn't believe it was. Bloomer's cheeks blushed crimson.

'Why are you acting so weird?' he asked.

'We didn't expect to see you,' Mr Davies explained. 'Dareth told us how upset you were about your mum.'

'Is she dead?' Sadiq enquired bluntly.

'Nah, she's fine,' Bloomer grinned.

'But what about the pains and stuff?' Jordan wanted to know.

Bloomer's grin widened. 'She was pregnant,' he said happily. 'She's had a baby.'

Suddenly the room erupted with noise and speech and laughter.

'She's had a baby! She's had a baby! Bloomer's mum's had a baby!' Max chorused, throwing himself around the room.

'But how?'

'What about...?'

'Is it a boy or girl?'

The questions tumbled from everyone's lips as Bloomer quickly got changed. Apparently his mum hadn't known she was pregnant. She hadn't planned to have a baby and she hadn't felt like she had when she'd had Bloomer and she hadn't put on lots of weight.

'So she's not fat like Kyle then,' Sadiq remarked. For once Kyle was too involved in Bloomer's story to rise to the taunt.

'The baby's come early,' Bloomer said, strapping on his shin-pads. 'They had to put him in one of those thingybobs 'cos he's mature.'

'What, like cheese?' Dareth queried.

'He means the baby's *pre*mature,' Mr Davies intervened. 'He must be in an incubator.'

'Yeah, that's it,' said Bloomer, pulling on a

sock. 'But they say he's fine, just a bit small.'

'Must run in the family,' said Jordan with a smile.

'A baby boy!' Max crowed, then waggled his hands in the air as if playing a trumpet.

Bloomer frowned. 'No, he's not a boy. He's a girl.'

'Bloomer, you der,' said Jordan with a pitying shake of her head. 'How can *he* be a *girl*?'

'Oh, yeah,' said Bloomer, pushing his foot into a boot. 'Well babies all look the same when they're tiny, don't they?'

There was a knock at the door.

'Hello!' a man's voice called. 'Are you decent? Can we come in?'

The door opened slowly and Max's dad's face appeared.

'Sorry to interrupt your team meeting,' he said. 'But I've got an important visitor out here who wants to meet you.'

'It's the Queen!' Max cried and the others laughed.

'Don't be daft, Max,' chided his dad. He stepped into the room, followed by a tall, thickset man with a ruddy complexion and a wide smile.

'This is Mr Marchant, boys, the chairman of the Doorstep Dairy. He introduced Mr Marchant to Mr Davies and they shook hands.

'I think we should show Mr Marchant our appreciation for sponsoring us. Well, Dareth?'

'Yeah,' Dareth agreed. He raised his thumb. 'Cheers, mate.'

'How about giving Mr Marchant three proper cheers?' Mr Davies suggested. 'Hip, hip...'

'... hooray!'

'Hip, hip...'

'... hooray!'

'Hip, hip...'

'... hooray!'

Mr Marchant looked pleased but a little embarrassed. 'Thank you,' he said. 'Good luck.'

Dareth's response took him by surprise. 'Hang an earl Big Ben yo!' he uttered. He looked at Sung-Woo.

'Hungunul Beegenyo,' the striker pronounced carefully. 'It mean 'good luck' in Korean.'

'Oh, good,' said Mr Marchant.

'Amazing what you learn at a football match,' Max's dad remarked wryly.

He and Mr Marchant walked to the door. The dairy chairman was just about to step outside when he turned and said, 'You know, you look just like Brazil in those shirts. I hope you play like them. Up the Bad Boyz!'

The responding roar almost blew Mr Marchant and Max's dad out of the changing room.

Mr Davies looked up and mouthed a silent thank you. Bad Boyz were a united team again!

9

Terminators kicked off and were the stronger team in the opening minutes. They had a very dangerous and tricky player up front, Asif, who was quick and strong and difficult to tackle. Fortunately for Bad Boyz his early runs were out wide and he had no real support in the middle.

Meanwhile Bad Boyz were struggling to get into any rhythm. They had barely had any time to warm up and started the match shakily. They seemed to be trying too hard – Dareth and Sung-Woo in particular. Every time they got the ball, they ran with it and took on opponents rather than passing. Terminators were very strong in defence, playing with three players at the back, so even if Dareth or Sung-Woo got past a couple of defenders there was always another one there to stop them. They just couldn't get past the last man.

Surprisingly, however, it was Bad Boyz who scored first. Sung-Woo ran on to a long ball clearance by Sadiq and shot early. It wasn't one of his best efforts and the keeper seemed to have it well covered. But somehow he let the ball slip through his legs and into the goal.

'Unlucky, son! Keep your head up!' called Mr Marchant kindly.

'And your legs together,' Max's dad added quietly.

To their credit, Terminators continued to take the game to Bad Boyz – and still looked the more dangerous team. Asif hit the post and then shot straight at Kyle when clean through on goal.

But it was only a matter of time before Terminators equalised; they were having all the play. Near the end of the first half, Asif took the ball past Jordan and then dummied to go outside Max, cutting into the penalty area instead. Wrong-footed, Max tripped him up. It was a clear penalty – well, clear that is, to everyone except Sadiq!

'That was a dive, ref!' he complained.

Asif took the kick himself and scored. Kyle got a hand to the shot but it was too powerful and he couldn't keep it out.

'Good effort, son!' Mr Marchant called. He was really into this match – as were all the spectators. It was gripping stuff.

At last the whistle blew for half-time. While the players sucked their oranges, Mr Davies gave them a pep talk.

'Let's get our passing game going,' he urged. 'Dareth, Sung-Woo, heads up when you've got the ball. Assess your options. Look for the player in space.' He told Jordan and Bloomer to push forward a bit to put more pressure on the Terminators' defence. The instruction to Max and Sadiq was to try to keep Asif out wide as they had done at the start and not let him run in on goal.

Bad Boyz began the second half much better. They were passing the ball quickly and causing Terminators more problems. They made a number of good chances in the first five minutes, but missed them all – Sung-Woo being the main culprit. They looked like being costly misses too, because soon after, the Terminators' goalie booted the ball clear and Asif sprinted past both Max and Sadiq, dribbled round Kyle and shot into an empty net. Were Terminators going to snatch the title from Bad Boyz right at the death?

'Come on, Bad Boyz!' Mr Davies called.

'Show them what you're made of, boys!' cried Mr Marchant eagerly. 'This is very exciting, isn't it?' he said to Max's dad with a smile.

'Too exciting,' said Max's dad with a shake of his head.

Bad Boyz responded well. They put together some really good moves. Jordan and Bloomer made some excellent runs down the flanks. At last, Bad Boyz were stretching the Terminators' back line.

Chances came – and went. On another day, Sung-Woo might have had a hat-trick in the second half alone. He hit the post, shot narrowly wide and missed his kick entirely right in front of goal. Dareth had a fine shot saved and Jordan saw an effort cleared off the line. It started to look as if Bad Boyz would never score. Then, midway through the half, Dareth was brought down in the penalty area. The referee pointed to the spot. Dareth laced the ball and walked back.

Mr Davies could hardly bear to watch.

The referee blew his whistle. Dareth trotted forward and kicked the ball. He didn't hit it cleanly, but the ball rolled towards the corner of the net. The goalie was well beaten. It looked like a certain goal – but no! The ball bounced against the post and straight into the goalie's arms. Dareth put his head in his hands. He couldn't believe it – and neither could the spectators!

'I don't think I could take this every week,' sighed Mr Marchant.

'No,' Max's dad agreed.

Mr Davies was speechless. It seemed like it just wasn't going to be Bad Boyz day.

Moments later Terminators almost increased their lead. Asif fired in a scorching volley that appeared destined for the top corner – but somehow Kyle got one of his giant hands to it and pushed the ball away for a corner. Then he bawled at his defenders for not covering properly.

'That's the spirit,' cooed Mr Marchant approvingly.

Bad Boyz attacked again and again, but still Terminators held firm. There were just five minutes left – and still no breakthrough. It looked as if Bad Boyz would have to settle for being runners-up.

With three minutes left, Max decided to go on the charge. He went through two tackles and carried on running. There were four Bad Boyz players ahead of him now and only three Terminators' defenders back.

'Pass it, Max!' shrieked Dareth.

But Max didn't seem to hear. He ran on towards goal and tried to go past another defender. This time he was tackled. But the ball fell kindly for Sung-Woo and he shot first time. He scuffed his shot rather and the keeper got a hand to the ball, parrying it to one side ... right in the path of Bloomer! Time seemed to stand still as Bloomer moved forward, lifted his left foot and kicked the ball ... straight into the back of the net!

'YES!' Bad Boyz had equalised at last! It was 2-2. The players went wild. They chased Bloomer and leapt on him. Then Max crossed his arms in front of him and started rocking them, as if he were rocking a baby – and the others joined in. All seven players ran to the touchline and stood in front of Mr Davies and his fellow spectators carrying out their odd goal celebration, which had changed now to putting their raised thumbs between their lips as if sucking on the teat of a baby's bottle.

'The goalscorer, Bloomer, has got a new baby sister,' Mr Davies explained between chuckles.

As it happened, there was soon further cause for celebration. A minute later, Bad Boyz scored again with an excellent team move, in which every player was involved. Kyle threw the ball to Sadiq, who passed to Max. He knocked the ball wide to Jordan, who flicked it first time to Dareth. He raced past one opponent before sliding a pass out to Bloomer on the left wing. A quick sprint and a cross and the ball was at the feet of Sung-Woo running in on goal. Without breaking stride, the striker lashed the ball high into the net. And that was it! Bad Boyz had won the game and were champions of the first half of the Appleton Little League.

Mr Davies watched them charging around the field like sugar-fuelled cheetahs, chanting 'Champions! Champions!' and he smiled. How much things had changed in such a short time! It seemed like just moments ago all had been doom and gloom and now everything was wonderful. One thing was for sure, life was never dull with Bad Boyz.

'Congratulations! That last goal was a beauty,' Mr Marchant enthused, shaking Mr Davies's hand. The dairy chairman's ruddy face beamed with pleasure. 'Just like Brazil, in fact....'

Appleton Little League Half-Season Table

Teams	Played	Won	Drawn	Lost	For	Against	Points
Bad Boyz	7	6	0	1	29	11	18
Hornets	7	4	3	0	22	8	15
Terminators	7	4	1	2	25	9	13
Dorking Runners	7	3	3	1	16	14	12
Vinnie's Vulcans	7	3	1	3	19	12	10
Eddy's Eagles	7	1	3	3	15	17	6
X Club 7	7	0	2	5	5	25	2
Dart United	7	0	1	6	3	38	01

The Complete Results of the First Half of the Appleton Little League

Week 1

Bad Boyz	4	v	Vinnie's Vulcans	2
Terminators	2	v	Hornets	2
Dorking Runners	3	v	X Club 7	1
Dart United	0	v	Eddy's Eagles	4

Week 2

Bad Boyz	5	v	Dorking Runners	2
Vinnie's Vulcans	6	v	X Club 7	0
Hornets	1	v	Eddy's Eagles	1
Terminators	9	v	Dart United	0

Week 3

Bad Boyz	7	v	Dart United	0
Vinnie's Vulcans	3	v	Eddy's Eagles	2
Dorking Runners	2	v	Terminators	1
Hornets	4	v	X Club 7	1

Week 4

Bad Boyz	5	**v**	Eddy's Eagles	3
Vinnie's Vulcans	6	**v**	Dart United	1
Hornets	3	**v**	Dorking Runners	3
Terminators	5	**v**	X Club 7	0

Week 5

Bad Boyz	4	**v**	X Club 7	0
Hornets	8	**v**	Dart United	0
Vinnie's Vulcans	1	**v**	Dorking Runners	1
Terminators	4	**v**	Eddy's Eagles	1

Week 6

Bad Boyz	3	**v**	Hornets	2
Terminators	2	**v**	Vinnie's Vulcans	1
Dorking Runners	2	**v**	Eddy's Eagles	2
X Club 7	1	**v**	Dart United	1

Week 7

Bad Boyz	3	**v**	Terminators	2
X Club 7	2	**v**	Eddy's Eagles	2
Hornets	2	**v**	Vinnie's Vulcans	0
Dorking Runners	3	**v**	Dart United	1

Follow Bad Boyz on their Little League cup run in the third book of this series.

K.O. Kings

Turn the page to read the first chapters.

1

'Catch it, Kyle, you big blob!'

The Bad Boyz keeper turned and glared at the shouting figure on the touch-line. He'd just palmed a fierce shot round the post and he reckoned it had been a pretty good save.

'Don't take any notice,' said Jordan. She clapped a hand on Kyle's broad shoulder. 'That was wicked.'

'Who is that geezer, anyway?' growled Sadiq, waving a clenched fist towards the touch-line.

'Yeah, who's he calling a big blob?' said Max. 'Great ugly gorilla.' He put his hands in his armpits, pulled a face and started making gorilla noises. Next to him Bloomer squeaked with laugher and joined in. They were still monkeying around when the corner came over. Luckily Dareth, the captain, was paying attention to the game and booted the ball clear.

'Come on, Bad Boyz! Concentrate!' called Mr Davies. He was both the Bad Boyz manager and a teacher at their school. He glanced along the touch-line. He was used to being his team's only supporter and he wondered who the man was who'd shouted at Kyle.

Mr Davies had never seen him before, but he was obviously someone who knew Kyle well. All his comments had been directed at the keeper – and none had been complimentary. Fortunately, Kyle was in a pretty good mood. The match was almost over and he hadn't let in a goal. At the other end, Bad Boyz had struck three times and were well set for a comfortable win.

It was the first round of the Appleton Little League Cup. Bad Boyz' opponents were X Club 7. In his pre-match team talk, Mr Davies had called them 'the most improved team in the league'.

'Yeah,' Dareth had agreed. 'But they're still pants.'

They'd looked anything but pants in the first half, though. The game had been very even and Kyle had had to make a number of fine saves – though none of them good enough for the man on the touch-line, it seemed. When Kyle parried the ball, he should have caught it; when he saved with his feet, he should have used his hands; when he booted the ball clear, he should have picked it up....

By half-time, only one goal had separated the teams – and that had been a fluke. A corner from Jordan had rebounded off the post, hit a defender on the heel and bounced back over the line.

In the second half, though, Bad Boyz had been well on top. Sung-Woo, their main striker, had scored twice and could have got three or four more. Jordan had hit the post with a scorching shot and Dareth had had a header cleared off the line.

To their credit, X Club 7 carried on battling to the end, even though they were obviously very tired. It was due to this tiredness that they gave away a penalty in the last minute. A weary defender stumbled and tripped Sung-Woo as the striker chased a long kick from Kyle. It was a clear penalty.

Dareth offered the ball to Sung-Woo. 'You take it,' he said. 'Get your hat-trick.'

But Sung-Woo shook his head with a

characteristic frown. 'You the penalty taker,' he insisted. 'I have two goals already. You score.'

Dareth shrugged. 'All right. Cheers!' he said.

He placed the ball on the spot and took a couple of steps backwards. Then he trotted forward and blasted it into the top right-hand corner of the net. At once he wheeled round and began his latest celebration. This involved cupping one hand round his ear and flapping the other like a wing. He was well into this before he noticed that no one else was joining in. They were all just standing looking at him.

Dareth's hands dropped and so did his smile. 'Wassup?' he said, puzzled.

Jordan nodded towards the goal. 'Look,' she said.

Dareth turned. The referee was still standing by the penalty spot with his arms folded. 'Take it again,' he ordered. 'And this time, wait till I blow my whistle.'

'I thought you did blow,' said Dareth.

The referee shook his head.

Dareth grinned. 'Must have been Bloomer, then,' he said.

Once more he placed the ball on the penalty spot.

Once more he took a couple of steps back.

He waited.

The referee blew his whistle.

Once more, Dareth ran forward and blasted the ball … but this time into the top left-hand corner.

He raised his hands and started to turn, but before he could, Bloomer and Max had jumped him. A moment later, Kyle tumbled on top and all four fell in a screeching heap.

The mystery man on the touch-line was not amused. 'Get back in goal, Kyle, you idiot!' he barked. 'The game's not over!' But he was wrong. For at that instant the referee blew the final whistle.

Bad Boyz had beaten X Club 7 by 4-0 – the same score as in the league. They were through to the next round of the cup.

2

'Who was that bloke?' asked Jordan when Bad Boyz were back in the changing room.

'What a pain in the butt,' said Max. 'Kyle, get back in goal,' he mimicked in a ridiculous husky voice. 'Pick the ball up, catch that cross, stop scratching your nuts.'

'Yeah, what was his problem anyway?' Sadiq added.

'Is he a relative or sumfing?' Dareth asked.

Kyle's small eyes narrowed to tiny dots. 'Yeah,' he huffed. 'He's me dad, ain't 'e.'

The others all stared at Kyle. But no one said anything. They'd heard about Kyle's dad.

'I thought he was in prison,' Dareth muttered finally.

'They let him out, didn't they,' said Kyle resentfully. 'Now he's come back round here to cause trouble.'

'Can't your mum do anything about it?' Jordan suggested.

Kyle shook his large head with resignation. 'She can't do nuffing. She's scared of him, ain't she. Everyone is.'

'I'm not,' said Sadiq defiantly.

'Yeah, well, that's cos you're a wally,' said Kyle. 'My dad 'ud rip yer 'ead off.' He punched his goalie top into his kit-bag.

The door opened and Mr Davies came in.

'Well played, everyone,' he said. His cheeriness died away at the sight of the gloomy faces before him. 'What's up?' he asked.

'It's him out there,' said Jordan.

'Yeah, who is he?' Mr Davies enquired. 'It's the first time I've seen him round here.'

'He's Kyle's dad,' said Jordan.

'They let him out of prison,' said Max.

' 'e's 'ard,' piped Bloomer.

'Well, he was certainly hard on you, Kyle,' said Mr Davies consolingly. 'I thought you had a brilliant match.'

'He don't think I'm no good at nuffing,' Kyle grumbled. 'He never has. Not that he can talk. The only fing he's any good at is makin' trouble.'

'Well, maybe you should stay away from

him,' said Mr Davies. 'Unless you *want* to see him, of course,' he continued quickly. 'He is your dad after all.'

'I don't want to have nuffing to do with him,' Kyle huffed. He tugged the zip on his bag and walked towards the door. 'I hate his guts.'

Mr Davies looked after his keeper anxiously. Trouble was never far away from Bad Boyz and he had a feeling it was about to pay them another visit.